TURKEY FOR CHRISTMAS

TURKEY
FOR
CHRISTMAS

Written and Illustrated by
MARGUERITE DE ANGELI

THE WESTMINSTER PRESS
Philadelphia

LIBRARY OF CONGRESS CATALOG CARD No. 65–10367

PUBLISHED BY THE WESTMINSTER PRESS®

PHILADELPHIA, PENNSYLVANIA

PRINTED IN THE UNITED STATES OF AMERICA

To
Nina
Arthur
Harry
and
Walter

And
To
Johnnie
Who
wasn't
There

TURKEY FOR CHRISTMAS

So," said Papa, "it comes down to this: either we have a few small gifts or we can have turkey for Christmas. We can't have both. Now, which do you choose?"

He looked first to Bess. Bess, because she was the one who would mind the most. Bess, who jumped up and down with joy when things went well, who felt the deepest woe when they didn't.

They all sat around the table after supper, that is, all except Martha. Bess was thirteen, Ben, eight, Eddy, six, and the baby, Johnny. Martha, fifteen, was in the hospital—had been there for almost six weeks.

"But why?" queried Bess. "Why?"

And the boys echoed, "Why?"

But Johnny said, "Turkey! Turkey!" clapping his hands.

Ben and Eddy added their voices to Johnny's, and Bess

7

said ruefully, quietly, "It wouldn't be Christmas without turkey." The wonder of Christmas was still to Bess some kind of blue-and-gold mystery.

Papa laid his hand over Bess's. "Bess, you are old enough to know that things don't happen by magic. They have to be worked for. It cost a great deal for us to move from Michigan to Philadelphia. Then Martha had to be cared for. Nurses and doctors must be paid. It costs a lot of money to run a hospital, to feed the patients, heat the building, keep it clean. It doesn't just happen. We have to pay our share. There are five of you to feed and buy shoes for. Do you realize that about every two weeks one of you needs a pair of shoes? And most often it is you!"

Bess nodded. "Yes," she murmured, "I never thought."

"We must think of the real meaning of Christmas," said Mamma, answering Papa's questioning look with her quiet smile. It was settled. They would have the usual Christmas dinner with turkey and everything that went with it, but there would be no presents.

"No new books?" said Bess.

"No," Mamma answered. "But there is still the library."

Bess nodded, but thought to herself, No sleds or skates, no windup toys to go click-clicking over the floor, and *no doll*. But as soon as she thought of that, she quickly remembered that she was too old for dolls anyway.

There were not even the usual homemade things, such as workbags and pincushions, because Mamma had no time to make them. One day Mamma had found pieces of silk and lace for Bess to make sachet bags. Mamma had only begun to show her how to fold and sew a heart-shaped one when the sudden, hurried call had come from the hospital. Martha had taken a turn for the worse. For days Mamma and Papa had spent most of the time with her, and the sachet bag had been forgotten. Once Bess had tried to make it by herself, but the slippery silk frayed at the edges. It seemed too hard to fold neatly. Besides, there was no sachet powder to put in it. It lay unfinished in the drawer.

"Will Martha come home for Christmas?" Bess asked.

"It is doubtful," said Papa, taking out his pipe and filling it.

"I *wish* she would. The table looks empty without her, and I don't like sleeping on that third floor alone. It's lonesome."

"Even if she is not home for Christmas," said Mamma, lifting Johnny from his high chair, "we still *have* her, and perhaps in a week or two she will be home."

"Yes," Papa agreed, "we are still a whole family, with no break in it. Everything else is unimportant. I am fortunate too in having this new territory for my work. Martha has had the best treatment we have been able to find and will soon be well."

Bess thought of all the good times she and Martha had had together. How well Martha played the piano for Bess to sing, when they made believe they were having an opera. She remembered how Martha always did what she was supposed to do, properly, with no shirking, no putting off on someone else what she was asked to do. A slow red crept over Bess's face as she remembered that day last winter. She had slipped out of the back door to go sledding down Catholic Hill in Michigan when Mamma had left both girls to care for the smaller children for an hour or so. She looked sadly at her disfigured thumb, which would always be a reminder of that day. On her first flight down the hill, she had crashed into a tree, crushing her thumb where it held on to the sled. She had run home crying, dreading Martha's scolding. But Martha had said not a word; she had done her best to care for the injury till Mamma had come home.

Bess could hardly believe she had often quarreled with Martha, mostly about the dishes and whose turn it was to wash.

If only she will come home and be well, she promised herself, I will never again quarrel about doing my share. I will never again borrow her collars or handkerchiefs without asking. I will dust the wooden shutters when it is my turn to clean our room, and I will keep my side of the bureau drawer straight and orderly.

As Bess began to put these secret resolutions to work by getting up to clear the table, Papa said, "There won't be any package for Grandma and Grandpa either. But we will write them a Christmas letter. They realize how hard it has been for us since we came east—the expense of moving and of Martha's illness. They know, too, how anxious we have been and how the concern about Martha has taken all our time and thought. They will understand."

"No package for Grandma and Grandpa?" asked Bess, looking ready to cry. A dull, sick feeling reminded her that she hadn't finished the sachet. That, at least, she could have done, if only she could have made herself stick to it and do it as carefully as Mamma had taught her.

"I guess there will be no package from them either," she said wistfully, remembering how they loved to open Grandma's package. It always smelled of plum pudding when it was opened. Now there would be no small bundles tied with saved-up paper and string. No kitchen holders for Mamma made from Grandma's piece basket.

"Well, we'll see," said Papa.

Bess thought of the things that might have been in that box as she gathered the dishes from the table and carried them to the kitchen. She heated the water without being told, and filled the dishpan.

Mamma took the baby to bed. The boys went to play in the upstairs sitting room, and Papa came to get the dishcloth to wipe off the high-chair tray. Now that it was settled about Christmas, he looked content, with his pipe sending a wreath of smoke about his head. He came back to the kitchen and began to dry the dishes Bess had washed. The smoke floated in a blue haze as it had done that Sunday morning several days after they had taken Martha to the hospital. She remem-

bered how Papa had come home and told the family that Martha was out of danger and would get well. He had lighted his pipe and helped Mamma to get dinner. Mamma had hummed to herself as she put the biscuits into the oven, and the world had seemed safe again.

Since then the news about Martha had been sometimes good and sometimes not so good. She improved slowly. When she was allowed to go see Martha, Bess had been terrified by the quiet efficiency of the special nurse. She had been allowed to stay only a few moments, and even as she had told Martha about the cat's chasing a stray dog up the alley, it had hurt Martha to laugh, and Bess had become frightened.

"Martha still needs special care," Papa began, "but the dreadful anxiety is over, thank goodness. He closed one eye to keep the smoke out, and went on, "We can do lots of things to keep the Christmas spirit. It is not the gifts, nor the turkey, that make Christmas. You know that. Besides, we can invite some lonely person to share our dinner. Perhaps that new young lady at the office, Miss Stevens. She has no one nearby."

"Yes, I know," answered Bess. "But it is exciting to find surprises like books and toys." She sniffed a little. "And we don't know Miss Stevens. Is she nice?"

"Very nice," said Papa, "and very lonesome."

"Remember how we used to go to Grandma's?" Bess went on. "There was always a tree in the parlor, as if it had grown there. Grandpa used to light all the candles, and there were tiny packages tied all over the tree. Remember?"

"Remember? Of course! It was always like that in my boyhood. Certainly I remember. But now that I am older, I wonder why the tree didn't take fire and burn up. It was never left alone, though, when the candles were burning."

"Christmas!" said Bess softly.

As always, the word had a special quality. A quality of mystery and magic—a vision of starry sky and the angelic choir, of the Babe in the manger. A baby who looked like Johnny. The vision was somehow tied up with the secrets the girls had shared with Mamma. A warm nightshirt for Papa, hurriedly hidden when he came home for supper. Chintz bags, with ribbon run through the casing, for Cousin Mary and for Grace. White lawn aprons for Grandma when she had high tea.

This year, with no girl to help in the kitchen, going to the hospital nearly every day after Bess came from school, Mamma had been too busy to make gifts. At night she was so tired she often fell asleep before the children went to bed, and Papa would tuck them in.

Martha and Bess were supposed to wash the supper dishes,

take care of their own room on the third floor, and help with the cleaning on Saturdays, while Mamma did the baking. Bess liked scrubbing better than dusting but often dawdled and put off starting work till Mamma's patience wore out. Martha had usually done her own work while Bess mooned over something she was reading or drawing and sometimes did Bess's share too.

Now Bess was so frightened at Martha's being ill enough to be in the hospital that she worked willingly, trying to make up for past carelessness and hoping that her wordless prayers for Martha's recovery would be answered. Still, she often forgot to make her bed, left cooking pots to soak overnight, and sometimes idled on her way home from school. It was hard to remember to be good.

Papa went on talking as he polished the plates and put them up in the cupboard. "We'll do something to let Grandma and Grandpa know we are thinking of them." He puffed on his pipe a moment. Then, "I have an idea! You'll see!" he said cheerily.

The leaden feeling in Bess's stomach suddenly lightened. The wonder returned. The feeling of crisp cold and starlight, of bells chiming! It no longer seemed important that on Christmas Eve there would be no packages to wrap, and on Christmas morning, no bulging stocking and mysterious

16

bundles. Suddenly company, even strange company for Christmas dinner, was exciting. She would help Mamma put the best dishes on the table, there would be a handsome turkey, and soon Martha would be home. They would be together again.

"Perhaps I can finish the sachet heart if I try," she said. "And you could take it to Martha."

"She would like that," Papa agreed, "and it would please Mamma. You so often begin things that you never finish. That is something you must learn."

"Yes," said Bess, "I will try."

Determined to neglect nothing, she put away everything as Papa dried the last cup and hung the tea towel on the rack. She drew the curtain across the window, brushed up the crumbs around the table, then followed Papa upstairs to the sitting room. She found the silk and lace, the needle and thread, and set to work.

Ben and Eddy were in bed, though they could still be heard squabbling over who had the most covers. As usual, their stockings were left for Mamma to mend.

Bess struggled with the seam of the satin heart. It pulled askew when she sewed it, and the threads frayed out in a fringe. Besides, a book of Andersen's fairy tales stood enticingly near on the table. She gave up the sewing and put the

17

heart back into the drawer. Before she began to read, she went to see what Papa was doing at the desk. He looked pleased with himself as he scribbled something on a piece of paper. Bess remembered what he had said in the kitchen. "Can I see what you are doing?" she asked, peeking over his shoulder.

"Wait. Wait," he said, covering it with his hand. So Bess sat down to read.

The coal fire in the grate hissed and sputtered. The gas lamp glowed white. To Bess it seemed as if she had hardly begun to read *The Tinder Box,* when Mamma looked up and said, "Bess, it's late. Go to bed."

"Wait a moment," Papa said. "See how this sounds." He began to read in rhyme the letter he had planned for Grandpa and Grandma's Christmas. "This is the first draft, of course."

In the letter he poked gentle fun at Grandma's habit of telling Grandpa how to carve the turkey, at Aunt Miriam for polishing off the bones, and at Grandpa for saving one little part for himself.

He read:

> *"Watch well where mother's finger points*
> *(You know you never carved before);*
> *Otherwise, you'll miss the joints—*
> *And don't spill stuffing on the floor.*

And:

"You know a trick worth two of that!
  When all the plates have been repassed,
I see on yours, with a bit of fat,
  The part that went over the back fence last!"

Here and there among the verses Papa had made small sketches that illustrated them. They were not much more than scribbles, but Bess could tell what they were supposed to be. Grandpa's chin whiskers and big nose told who *he* was. The strutting turkey looked proud, not knowing how soon he was to lose his head. There was a plum pudding, with curly steam rising from it, and a Christmas tree covered with the gifts they would like to send but couldn't.

How they laughed at the fun in the verses and at the drawings, but back of the laughter there was always a catch in the throat!

"They will love it," said Mamma, her gray eyes shining.

As Bess lay in bed thinking of the Christmas letter and how much fun they'd had listening to it, she thought again of Martha and wished she had heard it too. She thought of Christmas Eve and how she would miss the giggling and whispering, with the thrill of expectant waiting. Christmas Eve was almost more exciting than Christmas itself. But this was to be a Christmas without presents. Not even to send to Grandma. The letter was to take their place. Would the

wonder be there just the same? What *was* the real wonder of
Christmas?

She thought of the first Christmas, of Mary, and the Gift
of God to the world, the Christ-child. A little shiver went
through her. She determined to finish the satin heart. She
could send it to Grandma. Grandma would be surprised that
she could sew. Or should it be for Mamma? Or Martha? She
fell asleep thinking of the tiny stitches she would use.

By morning light, Bess knew it had been snowing. A bright
radiance filled the room, and the sound of voices was different, gay—and carried by the wind.

When she came home from school, she intended to go
sledding with the boys, who were already out. Mamma was
baking gingerbread men, and Johnny was watching from his

21

high chair. Bess put raisins on for eyes and buttons. She forgot about going out.

"A small package came today," Mamma said as she tested the cookies that were baking. "I haven't opened it. I thought we'd better save it for Christmas."

"Oh, *let's* open it!" cried Bess, clapping her hands as she always did. *"Let's!"*

"Not till Papa comes home, anyway. It is addressed to both of us, 'and Family,'" said Mamma, sprinkling cinnamon on the cookie men. "Bess, will you please bring the pail and wipe up the floor? I've spilled sugar and tracked it."

"Yes, Mamma," said Bess.

When Papa came home, Bess ran to meet him. "Oh, Papa, say we can open the package!" she begged. But Papa kept on walking through the long hall, walking Bess backward, his cold gloves on her shoulders making her teeth chatter. Or was it something else? Was it the sheaf of evergreens he carried that tickled her chin? Or was it the special look he gave Mamma as he kissed her? When he kissed Bess, he rubbed his cold cheek against her ear, warming himself before going to Johnny, who reached out to him. He and Mamma talked of the things that had happened during the day.

"One of the men in the office brought these greens from his home in New Jersey," Papa said. "Did the coal come?"

"Yes, thank goodness. We had only a few shovelfuls left. Did you stop at the hospital?"

"Yes," Papa said, and from the down-and-up sound of his voice, Bess knew that Martha was all right.

At that moment the boys came in, slamming the front and vestibule doors, drowning out what Papa was saying. They raced through the dining room to the kitchen, both sniffling with cold and tracking the floor with muddy snow.

Bess stamped her foot. "Why can't you wipe your feet!" she stormed. "I just washed this floor." But Ben paid no attention, running to the cellar to take some bit of trash he had found that might be of use in making something. Eddy looked at her and shrugged his shoulders.

"Temper! Temper!" said Mamma, shaking her head. Bess remembered her secret promises.

"Well," she said, "in Michigan, when winter comes, it stays. But here the snow soon melts and makes slush. We can't go sledding very often."

"Yes, it's true," answered Mamma soothingly. "But the cold is not so bitter, and it takes less to heat the house. Please set the table, Bess. It's time to get supper."

"Supper! Supper!" cried Johnny, banging his cup on the tray. The other boys were hungry too and clamoring for something to eat. There was so much noise and confusion that nothing more was said about the package, and Bess was sure it would have to be saved for Christmas. But Christmas was nearly here! And even while she wished for the package to be opened, she wanted it to be saved.

That evening, while Bess washed the dishes, Papa heated an iron and pressed the creases out of some brown wrapping paper kept in the cellarway. Bess watched and asked, "What is it for, Papa?"

"You'll see!" he said. When Papa folded it and cut it into even-sized pieces, she knew it was for the Christmas letter. "Why don't you work on the heart and get it done?" he suggested. "Yes," Bess agreed, "I will, and surprise Mamma."

The boys were in bed. The house was quiet at last. Mamma had done the mending and was cutting out a warm, pink bed jacket for Martha to wear when she sat up. Once again Bess got out the silk pieces and set to work. It went better this time, and she had sewed halfway round the edge before Mamma noticed what she was doing. Bess turned away to hide her work, and Mamma, understanding the way of secrets, went on with her own sewing.

Papa sat at the desk, copying the Christmas letter and the sketches onto the brown paper, using the girls' school paints to color the sketches. He decorated the front page with holly and showed the turkey, looking real enough to eat, served up in style with a sprig of green on his breast. The brown paper lent a color of its own and blended well with the paints Papa used. Mamma found a piece of red ribbon to thread through the holes punched along the side so it looked like a booklet. Then Papa hurried to get it mailed, and Bess knew it was too late to send the heart to Grandma. She would give it to Mamma. Even if it had no sweet smell, it would look nice among Mamma's handkerchiefs. Perhaps she could make another one for Martha.

"I hope the folks will enjoy this letter for what it is meant to be—a joke," Papa said as he sealed the wrapping.

"Oh, they will, I know," Mamma assured him.

"If only Martha could have been here to see it," Bess mourned. "When *will* she be home?"

"It's hard to say," Mamma said. "It might be in a week or so, if she continues to improve. It might be less. We hope so." She turned away, and Bess couldn't tell whether she was almost crying or almost laughing. Grownups had strange ways.

School was over early the next day. And then, suddenly, it was the day before Christmas! Bess knew it the moment she opened her eyes, for Papa was calling her, as he often did, with, "Breakfast is served in the dining car! Last call for breakfast!" Sometimes he banged on the frying pan to wake the sleepy girls. But when he called, "Breakfast in the dining car," they knew that it was a holiday or Sunday, or that there would be something special for breakfast.

Christmas Eve! thought Bess, jumping out of bed. Christmas Eve! It was still dark, but she knew by the blue glimmer in the square of the window that it had snowed again. Maybe there would be sledding! She shivered with excitement and with cold. There was little heat coming up to the third-floor bedroom. As she hurried into her clothes, she remembered that Papa would be home, and he was to have two weeks vacation at Christmas as well as in summer. He would help with the preparation for Christmas, and the work would be fun. The boys could play outside and not clutter up the house as fast as it was straightened.

Breakfast over, Papa said, "First, there is the basket to fill for someone who needs it. You boys can take it to the church on the sled. Mamma made an extra cake, and there's flour, sugar, cereal, and several jars of jelly she made last summer. And there's the chicken I brought from the market."

Bess helped pack the basket and thought how happy someone would be to open it.

When the boys had gone and she had cleared the table, Mamma came into the kitchen and said, "Wouldn't you like to take Johnny up and give him his bath?"

"Of course," Bess answered, thinking that now she wouldn't have to do dishes. Bess loved Johnny. She loved his dear softness. She often rocked and sang him to sleep, his head growing heavy on her shoulder.

"Be sure to keep him warm!" Mamma warned. "You'll find his clothes in the bottom drawer in the back bedroom. I have moved the boys' things up to the third floor. They're old enough to sleep up there." For a moment, Bess thought from Mamma's secret look that she might be hiding a surprise for Christmas; then she remembered that there would be no surprises for Christmas, except perhaps the small package that had come in the mail. Anyway, bathing Johnny was more fun than housework. It was almost like playing with a doll. She lifted him from his chair. It still seemed to be night in the dining room, with the gaslight burning and the shutters closed. But through the front door, as they passed, she could see the new snow sparkling bright in a gold-and-purple morning. Snow! And Christmas Eve! Bess flew up the stairs so fast with Johnny in her arms that Papa called, "Here, here! Not so fast!" But Johnny loved it and crowed with delight, hugging her tight to hold on.

As she passed the sitting room, Bess thought of the heart, and wished it were finished. There was still some of the edge to do and the lace to put on. If only she had something to make it smell sweet!

She tumbled Johnny on the bed after his bath and powdered him. The fragrance of the powder gave her an idea. Why not use powder for the sachet? Babies always smelled sweet. Right that moment she flew to the sewing table and took out the heart and ran back to Johnny just as he was getting off the bed.

Bess found his clothes as Mamma had said, in the back bedroom, but she went into Mamma's room to look for the buttonhook. She was surprised to find the bed made and everything in order. Mamma's room was always orderly, but now it looked spick-and-span, as if ready for company, and it was still early in the morning! There was a stiff, clean counterpane and fresh covers on the pillows, nothing hanging on the clothes tree, not even Papa's bathrobe. Mamma came into the room then with a large bouquet of chrysanthemums. Johnny paddled about in his stocking feet.

"Oh," said Bess, "how lovely! Is that Miss Stevens coming to spend the night?"

"Hardly," answered Mamma. "But perhaps she thought flowers would be nice for Christmas, and it is cooler up here, so they will keep well."

"Oh," said Bess. Once again she thought Mamma had a

strange look, as if she were keeping a secret. As for the tidiness of the room, Bess thought it was because there was so much to do on Christmas Eve.

When she brought Johnny down, bathed and dressed, to set him in his high chair to watch what was going on, she found dishes piled together but still unwashed, and Papa crumbling stale bread for stuffing. Mamma was at the table, taking pinfeathers out of the turkey's breast. They both laughed at Bess's rueful look as she eyed the dishes. "I thought they would be done," she said.

"Never mind," Mamma comforted her. "We'll all help, and it won't take long." Bess did not really mind, for at the moment, the kitchen was the nicest part of the house. It smelled of onion and sage, of the sharp tang of vinegar from the salad dressing cooking in the double boiler, and of the tart sweetness of cranberries bubbling beside it. Papa hummed as he crumbled the bread. He liked to cook, or at least he liked being in the kitchen with Mamma. As often happened when he started singing, Mamma and Bess joined in with soprano and alto parts. Of course Martha was not here to make it complete, but it was pleasant and part of home.

"The silver should be polished and the salts and peppers cleaned and filled," Mamma said, looking at Bess with her eyes twinkling.

"*Mamma,* you know how I hate the puckery feeling of silver polish!" Then she added, "But I do like to see it shiny when it's rubbed. And I like to get out the good dishes and set the table for company. Can I?"

"Of course, and we'll put on the long table cloth. But that must wait for tomorrow. Supper must be served tonight and breakfast tomorrow before that."

Bess skipped for the unexplainable joy that filled her. It was Christmas Eve!

By the time the silver was polished, the turkey was stuffed, the breast plumped out and sewed with a huge needle and string.

"There," said Mamma as she tied the legs together. "He's ready for the oven. I know it is better not to stuff the turkey the day before it is to be cooked, but my mother always did it and I always have." She was talking to Papa but looked at Bess as she spoke.

She covered the bird with a tea cloth and carried it out to the cold shed. The smell of evergreens came in when the door was opened, reminding them it was time to decorate the house. Papa laughed as he snatched off Bess's red hair ribbon and tied it with a branch of hemlock to the chandelier in the parlor. The rest of the greens they placed around the pictures, except for a spray they put into a vase on the square piano.

31

While Papa and Bess were still putting up the greens, the postman came. There was so much mail he had to wheel it around in a pushcart. Bess went to the door.

"Come, help!" she cried. "There are cards from everybody. Oh, and another package! It's from Grandma. They haven't forgotten after all!"

"Of course they wouldn't forget," said Papa, coming to help carry the things in. Bess could tell even before she saw the writing that Grandma had wrapped it. The outer cover was broken a little, and through it they could see bits of red paper and green string. There was probably a letter inside too. Grandma put in what she felt like putting in, not caring, if she knew, that letters must not be included in a package, not knowing that holders and lace collars always kept an odor of fruitcake and plum pudding.

But the packages were always exciting to open because each thing was wrapped separately, and there were always several things, no matter how small they might be, for each one. Sometimes they even got back what they had given Grandma the year before!

The letters and cards were filled with good wishes for Christmas and the New Year. Papa read them aloud and at times stopped and swallowed, especially when he came to the places that spoke of how anxious they all were about Martha.

The boys came in with wet, cold hands, and stockings bedraggled with snow. "Bess," Mamma said, "see that Ben and Eddy change into dry things and that they wash their feet in warm water first."

Bess started to protest; weren't they old enough to dress themselves? She remembered her new resolve to be obedient. "Yes, Mamma," she said, and went to help.

After lunch when they went out again with the sled, Mamma allowed Bess to go too.

"But you must come in when I call you to stay with Johnny while Papa and I go to see Martha."

"Christmas Eve and snow on the ground, and I have to stay in the house with Johnny?" she asked petulantly.

"Yes," said Mamma. "Remember, it is Christmas Eve for Martha too, and she *is* in the hospital." Bess nodded, ashamed of her selfishness.

The house was on a street where there was little traffic except for an occasional delivery wagon. The street ended at the upper corner, and they could sled all the way down past the house and into the block below. Every boy and girl in the neighborhood was in the street that afternoon. Jess and Charlotte were there, taking turns with Bess on her sled because it was so fast. Grandpa had made it for Bess the Christmas before, of chestnut wood. It was heavier and stronger than the "boughten" ones and lay close to the ground. Sometimes they coasted as far as the end of the next block. Sometimes they had collisions and fell laughing into the snow. It was fun, but the snow went up Bess's sleeves, which she had outgrown; it sifted down her neck and soaked through her worn mittens. She was glad to go in when Mamma called. Charlotte went in with her to stay awhile and get warm.

"Can we make popcorn?" Bess asked.

"Yes," Mamma consented. "You may, if you leave the kitchen as clean as you find it. Everything is ready for supper, and we will come home as soon as we can. Dress Johnny quickly when he wakes, that's a good girl."

Johnny was still asleep and didn't waken till the popcorn was half eaten. Charlotte and Bess sat before the fire in the sitting room talking about Christmas and their different ways of observing Christmas Eve, and the gifts they wished for.

"I want skates," said Charlotte, "and a heavy sweater and a new pair of mittens."

"I'd like—" Bess began, then stopped. She was about to say, "A doll," but thought in time, knowing that Charlotte would think her silly. She began again, "Mittens too, and a new nightie. Mine are getting short. And I'd like skates, now I know where the pond is." She didn't tell that there would be no presents. That was a family secret. But she did tell about the turkey Mamma had ready and the good things they would have with it. She showed Charlotte the heart, hoping she wouldn't guess that the perfume was bath powder.

While they talked, Bess finished sewing the lace on the edge.

"How can you make such fine stitches?" Charlotte wondered. "I can't sew at all." Bess knew the sewing was not so fine as Mamma's, but she had finished it, and Mamma would be pleased.

When Johnny woke, they dressed him and played with him. Charlotte asked him what he wanted in his stocking for Christmas, but he only said, "Turkey, turkey!"

Charlotte wanted to go sledding again before dark, so she went out, and Johnny and Bess were alone. Bess pulled him up into her lap. "Sing!" he said. "Sing!"

Bess made up a song story about the Babe in the manger, the shepherds, and the angels.

Johnny was quiet, looking into the fire as Bess did.

The house was still. Only the ticking of the clock on the mantel and a whisper from the glowing coals broke the quiet. It didn't seem at all like Christmas Eve. The heart sachet

was finished, but it seemed *very* little.

Why didn't I make another one for Martha? Bess thought. Soon it will be night—really Christmas Eve—then morning and Christmas! But no Martha, no presents, only turkey. Christmas night will come, and we'll have to wait a whole year till Christmas comes again. She felt sad. She wished Ben and Eddy would come in, even if they tracked up the vestibule, even if they were noisy. She wished Mamma would come home, and Papa. It would seem more like Christmas Eve. And oh, she wished Martha were home!

Johnny yawned. Bess could hear, faintly, the sounds of the boys and girls coasting down the street.

"Let's go watch the boys, shall we?" She lifted Johnny, keeping him close.

"Boys! Boys!" cried Johnny, trying to get down. Bess set him on the floor, guarding him against the stairs.

Just then she heard the door click.

Was it Ben and Eddy?

Johnny looked down the stairs, then at Bess questioningly. "Boys?" he asked.

But the inner doors were opening! Papa's voice came through.

"Papa?" said Johnny.

Papa was unfastening the *double front doors*. Bess's heart began to beat.

What was happening?

Bess saw Mamma coming up the front porch steps. Following her was a young man in white. He looked like the doctors who had come for Martha!

He was leaning forward and was carrying something. Could it be—

It *was!* It was Martha! Martha on the stretcher. She was laughing! She was coming in the doorway and being carried up the stairs. She was almost well! She was home!

She turned her head to see Johnny and Bess, and caught Bess's hand as she passed.

"Hello, there!" she called out, but something kept Bess from speaking. She squeezed Martha's hand as she passed.

Ben and Eddy had come in to share the excitement, but for once they were quiet and talked in excited whispers.

Now Bess knew why Mamma had moved the boys to the third-floor back room. Now she knew why Mamma had had that secret look when Bess had asked about Martha and why her bed was ready for company. Martha was the company! And the flowers—they were for Martha too.

The boys let Bess help them get washed and take off their damp things and put them to dry. They went up to inspect their new room, tiptoeing and whispering as they went.

While Bess was putting the water on to boil for supper, Mamma came down to fix a tray for Martha.

"She is used to having supper early in the hospital and will be needing it after the excitement of coming home," Mamma said.

"Let me fix her tray. Oh, please, let me!" Bess begged.

Mamma found the things she had prepared for Martha and heated them while Bess brought a doily and arranged the dishes.

The whole family gathered around to watch Martha while she ate. From somewhere Papa had brought a tiny tree that stood in the corner by Martha's bed. She sat up to eat, and around her shoulders was the pink jacket. It did make her look pretty. The flowers stood on the bureau and doubled themselves in the mirror. A sleigh passed with bells jingling, and the boys flew to the window, remembering it was Christmas Eve. Suddenly Bess knew that the heart was for Martha after all. It would match her jacket.

Papa sent them all out of the room, but promised to read the Christmas story before bedtime.

Mamma let them hang up their stockings. "Just for fun," she said, "but there might be an orange in each one—if you are good, that is."

The two packages were brought up and put under the tree. All the stockings were hung at the foot of Martha's bed. Bess slipped the heart into the toe of Martha's stocking as she hung it up, and when the children were ready for bed, Papa read the Christmas story. Each year when the old, old story was read from the book of Luke, it seemed to Bess as if she was hearing it for the first time. This time the same wonder was there! The feeling that there was something so big inside her she could not contain it; something practically lifted her off her feet. Something really WONDER *full*.

40

Early next morning, she heard the boys running in their bare feet down the stairs to the second floor. She heard Mamma say, "SH-h-h-h," then heard Martha call, "I'm awake! Merry Christmas everybody!"

"Merry Christmas! Merry Christmas!" came from everywhere, and the whole family came together into Martha's room. Papa lighted the gas burner for extra warmth, and Mamma brought another blanket and set Johnny on the bed beside Martha.

The stockings along the end of the bed *did* have something in them—something more than oranges. But what funny things. Out of the top of the boys' stockings came two pairs of new ones. In Johnny's was a pair of shoes. In Martha's was a strange contraption like a belt that the doctor said she must wear for a while after she got out of bed. And far down in the toe beneath the orange was the sweet-smelling heart edged with lace.

"You finished it!" said Mamma in astonishment, but Bess thought Mamma was not as surprised as she pretended. Martha didn't say much more than, "Thank you, dear." But Martha never did say much. She never jumped up and down

42

as Bess did. But she looked pleased as she pinned the heart right over her own on the pink jacket.

In Bess's stocking there was a pair of long drawers that she badly needed and an orange like the rest had. If there had been skates and mittens, a doll and a bracelet, it would have been nice. But these homey things were more dear because with each was a rhyme, written as were those in the Christmas letter—just for fun.

Bess's read:

> *Here are the underdrawers,*
> *Warm and snug—*
> *You've needed them "long"*
> *So your ankles they'll hug.*

Bess laughed at the "long." Papa knew how long she had needed them.

After the oranges had been brought out of the stocking toes, Mamma said, "Now, you must dress and we'll have breakfast."

"Oh—before we open the packages?"

"Yes," said Papa. "The longer we wait to open them, the longer we have to wonder what is in them. Anticipation is more than half the fun. Scamper now!" And scamper they did.

When they were upstairs again in Martha's room, the morning was well advanced. The turkey was in the oven and already sending up its sagey smell. Papa fiddled around, calmly smoking his pipe, rearranging the flowers, asking Martha if she was comfortable, if she had enjoyed her breakfast—doing endless small things to tease instead of opening Grandma's package. Finally, even Johnny begged, "Open, open!" Papa picked it up and fussed with the string, humming through the pipe smoke, trying to undo the knots, till Mamma slipped up behind him with the scissors and snipped the cord.

At last! It was opened, and there were the packages of all sizes and shapes, none very large, but each tied separately with different kinds of ribbon and string, sending up an odor of brown sugar and spice, sachet powder and lavender.

Each package was marked for someone special in Grandma's spidery writing. There were holders for Mamma as always, this time in the shape of pigs, with curly tails to hang them by. There was a necktie for Papa of every color in the rainbow. When he saw it, he said to Mamma, "Well, it will look fine in that silk quilt you are making, Ruby." It didn't look like the ties Papa was used to wearing. In another package was a lace collar for Mamma and in still another, an apron with rickrack braid. In parcels for Martha and Bess were chains made of small beads sewn into daisy shapes, and in other parcels, a sewing bag for each, fitted out with needles and silver thimbles.

There were penknives for Ben and Eddy, and Bess heard Mamma whisper, "I only hope they soon lose them." There was a feeding bib for Johnny embroidered in red, and a rubber ball done up in tinsel. There were mouth organs for the boys, which they proceeded to play, each in his own tune and time.

There was a warm fascinator for Martha, and in another package for Bess, a soap baby wrapped in a washcloth. The very one she had given Grandpa the Christmas before!

Mamma picked up the small package that arrived first. "It's from my great-aunt Dicey," she said as she opened it. "I know her writing." As Mamma unwound the tissue, she said,

45

M.de A.

"I think I know what it is."

Bess leaned close. What could it be? But as the tissue fell away, it seemed hardly worth undoing. In it was an old bent spoon, longer than a teaspoon, not so large as a tablespoon or even a soup spoon. It was very shabby, though brightly shining. With it was a letter.

My dear niece,

This spoon belonged to your great-great-grandmother. It has been handed down from mother to daughter and sometimes from aunt to niece. Since I have no daughter to whom I may pass it on, I am sending it to you at this Christmas time, thinking that what it has been through will encourage you at this difficult time.

One Christmas, during the Revolution, your New England great-great-grandmother used it to ration out salt to the townspeople. Later, it was used by no less a person than General Washington, who was quartered with his staff in her niece's house in Pennsylvania. It has been lost in strange places. Once, after a year, it was found at the bottom of the swill barrel. Another time, during my childhood, it was gone for another year. When the well was cleaned out in the spring, there it was at the bottom.

From your great-aunt Louise, it went with my mother on her wedding journey to Michigan. I have heard her tell how that first Christmas found them with very little to eat because the crops had failed, the cow was sick, the roads piled high with snow, and I was a newborn Christmas baby. My father used this spoon to feed me the gruel he made from a mixture of wheat and oat grains he had ground on a stone.

47

She says they were able to laugh at their troubles on that Christmas Day because they had me. We were all strong and healthy, and there was the future to be happy in.

I scarcely know your family, my dear, but I am sure that it is as close-knit and fine as any of the family groups which this spoon has served for so long. I hope it will stir up happiness for you and yours, and bring you my love.

Aunt Ladicea

Bess looked at Martha with Johnny's bright head beside her. They each looked from one to another. Bess knew then the real meaning of Christmas. Love was in the look that passed among them. There was still company to come. There was still the turkey dinner. That would be fun. But this—the look that passed among them—*this* was the meaning of Christmas!